Ebb and Flo
and the Sea Monster

Jane Simmons

ORCHARD BOOKS

For Neil

ORCHARD BOOKS
96 Leonard Street, London EC2A 4XD
Orchard Books Australia
32/45-51 Huntley Street, Alexandria NSW 2015
First published in Great Britain in 2005
ISBN 1 84121 771 9
Text and illustrations © Jane Simmons 2005
The right of Jane Simmons to be identified as the author
and illustrator of this work has been asserted by her in accordance
with the Copyright, Designs and Patents Act, 1988.
A CIP catalogue record for this book is available from the British Library.
1 3 5 7 9 10 8 6 4 2
Printed in Singapore

Granny and Flo were reading the local newspaper. "That's Morgawr, our mystery sea monster," said Granny. "Lots of people say they have seen it, but this is the first picture."

"Morgawr the sea monster!" said Flo.

Ebb chewed her favourite ball.

Ebb sucked it,

and tossed it,

and nudged it.

But, oh! Ebb's ball
bounced right into
the bushes.

Ebb couldn't see her ball anywhere.
"Come on, Ebb! Time to go home or
we shall miss the tide!" called Mum.

"Ebb!" called Flo, but Ebb couldn't leave
without her favourite ball.

At last she found it.
"Woof! Woof!" barked Ebb, excitedly.
"Come on, we might still have time
to get across the bay," said Mum.
"Take this basket just in case,
and don't forget to look for
Morgawr!" said Granny.

On the way home, Flo watched out for sea monsters.
Ebb played with her ball, sucking it,
tossing it, and nudging . . . oh!

Splosh!
"Woof!" cried Ebb.
"Ebb's ball is in the water!"
said Flo.

Mum swung the boat around.

As Flo reached for the ball,
the boat hit the bottom.
"Oh no!" said Mum.

The boat was stuck, and slowly the tide went out.
"We're marooned!" said Mum.
"I'm hungry and I want to go home!" moaned Flo.

Ebb looked at her ball and wished
she hadn't dropped it.

"It will be alright. Look!
You can see our houseboat
from here," said Mum, as she
wrapped a blanket around Flo.
"Woof!" woofed Ebb.

"Let's get to the island," Mum said. "We'll collect sticks for a fire, and make a shelter, and use dry reeds for a bed. When the tide comes in, it's only a short ride home."

"What's in Granny's basket?" Mum asked.

"Hot chocolate and sausages and
lots more food!" said Flo, excitedly.
Ebb chewed her ball.

As darkness fell, the sounds of the night came alive. Owls hooted, the curlews cried, and the plip-plop of fishes jumping seemed to echo in the dark.

They ate supper, sang songs and watched big ships sailing into the distance.

"Have you seen Morgawr the sea monster?" asked Flo.
"No!" laughed Mum. "I think if there's a Morgawr, it
must be very shy."

Mum tucked Flo up in her blanket next to Ebb. "I'm going to look around for some more wood for the fire. I won't be far," said Mum, and she disappeared into the night.

Ebb played with her ball, tossing it and nudging . . . oh!

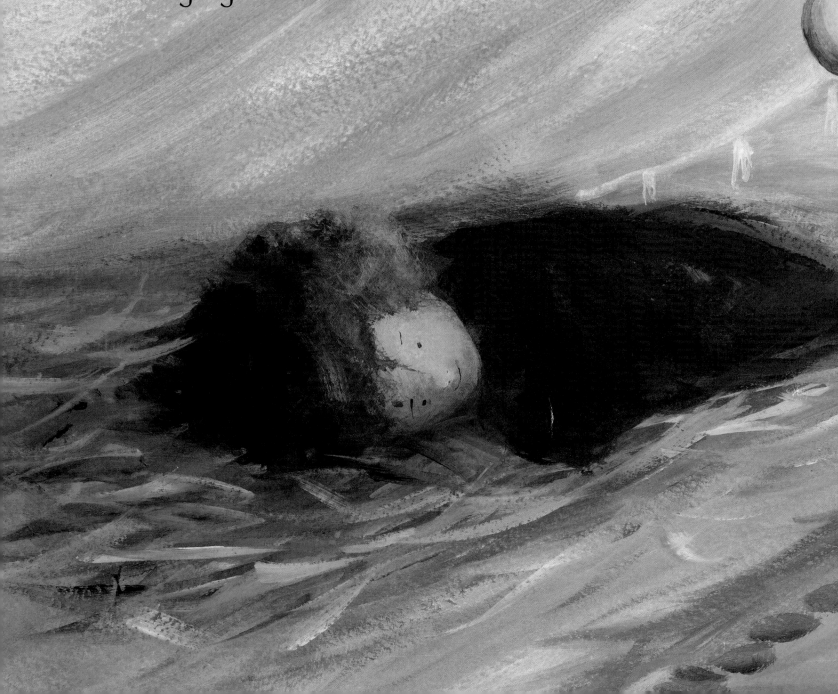

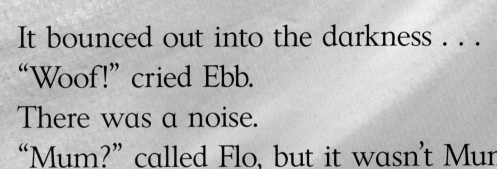

It bounced out into the darkness . . .
"Woof!" cried Ebb.
There was a noise.
"Mum?" called Flo, but it wasn't Mum.
Ebb saw the shadow . . .

The shadow grew bigger . . .
"GRRR!" growled Ebb.

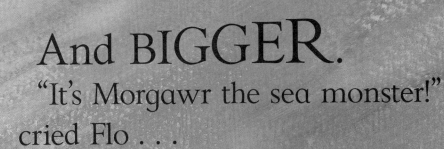

And BIGGER.
"It's Morgawr the sea monster!"
cried Flo . . .

"Beep!"
"Bird!" said Flo giggling. "Maybe Bird
is Morgawr the sea monster after all!"
"Woof!" went Ebb.

Ebb sucked her favourite ball,
and they all fell asleep
under the stars.

When the sun rose, the tide came in.
Ebb held her ball carefully and they
set off across the bay to home . . .

and no one noticed
anything strange.